DOCTOR · WHO

D0348349

THE DARKSMITH LEGACY

THE END OF TIME

BY JUSTIN RICHARDS

Book
10

The Darksmith adventure continues online. Log on to
the website, enter the special codes from your book
and enjoy games and exclusive content about
The Darksmith Legacy.

www.thedarksmithlegacy.com

Contents

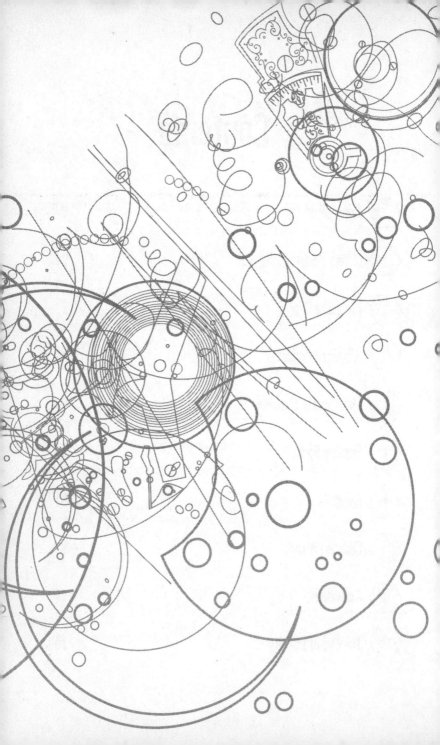

The Story So Far...

The Doctor has taken the powerful Eternity Crystal from the terrible Darksmith Collective on the planet Karagula and secretly replaced it with a fake. The Crystal can create life, and the Doctor knows it mustn't be allowed to fall into the wrong hands. The Darksmiths need the Crystal to fulfil their contract to create a terrible device for a mysterious client.

With the help of Gisella – the robotic 'daughter' of Varlos, the Darksmith who created the Crystal – the Doctor tries to find out who the Darksmiths are working for. The people who commissioned the Crystal are the only ones who know how to destroy it.

The mysterious clients are revealed: the dreaded Krashoks. With Gisella trapped on board their ship, they prepare to take off from Medieval England and return to their own time…

Every Cloud...

Blue lightning crackled in the winter air, lighting up the clouds and sending tendrils of energy dancing across the treetops.

'No, no, no!' The Doctor could only watch in horror as the Krashok ship faded into nothingness.

'They've gone.' Oswald shook his head in disbelief. 'The demons have gone.'

'Yes,' said the Doctor, his face grim. 'With Gisella trapped on board. And she has the real Eternity Crystal. If they find her then they find it.'

'What will you do?'

'Follow them. Try and catch up with them before they discover her.'

'But how will you know where they have gone?'

The Doctor shook his head. 'I don't know.'

A cry of pain made him turn. The witch had dropped to her knees, her eyes rolled back into her skull showing nothing but white, her body shaking in violent spasms.

The Doctor knelt before her as the shaking stopped. The witch's eyes snapped open. 'The demons have returned to the time from whence they came. Here they used the bodies of our children for their deeds, now they seek those with the keenest minds. Find the brightest of the young, Time Lord, and you will find your friend.'

'The brightest of the young? What does that mean?' The Doctor gripped her by the shoulders. 'Tell me!'

The witch shook her head. 'The writings tell me nothing more.' She hung her head, exhausted by her vision.

The Doctor stood, turning to Oswald. 'Will you take her back to the church, to Friar Meadows? Tell him that his novice needs somewhere better than a cave to live. That her mental gifts needs a better outlet than telling the future for a few rich nobles.'

Oswald nodded. 'I won't see you again, will I Doctor?'

The Doctor shrugged. 'Who knows Oswald. Perhaps when you are the greatest bard in all of England I'll come back and watch a gig. Backstage pass of course!'

The Doctor turned and made his way up the hillside, vanishing through the snow covered trees towards his waiting ship. Oswald watched him go. Already he had the making of a poem so epic that it would mark him down as having one of the foremost imaginations in the land.

All he had to work out now was how much he dared to tell.

The Doctor was not usually a pessimist. He was used to seeing the best in everything, and finding a silver lining to every cloud. But even he had to admit that things were looking pretty bad.

The Darksmiths might no longer be a problem. But that was because they'd finally delivered their commission to their mysterious clients. Those clients were the Krashoks – which meant things were just about as bad as they could be. And that was before you considered that the Krashoks now had a device that could bring their fallen soldiers back from the dead to fight again.

Silver lining time, the Doctor thought as he paced round the TARDIS console – first one way, then back the other. 'Come on, Doctor,' he said to himself. 'Things can't be *that* bad. Things are never *that* bad.'

The Krashoks might have the Eternity Device, but Gisella had sabotaged it. She had replaced the all-important Eternity Crystal with a fake, a copy. That was why the Doctor and Gisella had to stop the Krashoks using the device on Earth, because it would have exploded and taken planet Earth with it. They'd succeeded too – so there was another good thing.

But now the Krashoks had gone, and Gisella was with them and the Doctor had no way of knowing where their ship was headed, apart from a cryptic message from a medieval witch.

'Every silver lining has a cloud,' the Doctor decided.

This particular cloud was a thunder cloud if ever there was one. Not only was Gisella trapped on the Krashok ship, but she had the *real* Eternity Crystal with her. The Doctor had to assume the Krashoks would find Gisella. And when they found her, they would search her and find the Crystal. And when they found the Crystal they would realize the one they had was a fake, and they'd replace it with the real one, and activate their Eternity Device and bring back from the dead every

Krashok soldier who had ever lived and died…

Except…

The Doctor paused in mid-step. He slowly put his foot down, carefully so as not to disturb the thought he was in the middle of having.

Why hadn't they activated the Eternity Device already?

They had been short of power after their ship temporally shifted from medieval times back to the present day. But they couldn't pull that trick again. They were stuck in their own zone now – which narrowed things down. And their ship had powered up again and taken off. So now they had the energy to activate the device. But they hadn't done it.

Why not? What did they still need? 'The brightest of the young'? What could that mean?

'Think, Doctor. Think!'

He went through the process in his mind, pretending he was a Krashok. He had the device, ready and primed and calibrated so that it would only revive Krashoks. Otherwise it would bring back every life form that had ever died – like the dead of Mordane. Or even animate and give life to stuff that had never been alive at all. Like the dust on the moon.

Calibrated.

Maybe that was it. It was a faint hope, but a hope nonetheless. What if the Krashoks had betrayed and killed the Darksmiths before the device was calibrated? They could hardly go back to the Darksmiths for help now. The Darksmiths wouldn't have taken too kindly to having their leader Drakon and his envoys killed and not being paid.

Already the Doctor was accessing the TARDIS data banks, and racking his own memories. Where could the Krashoks go for the technical help they needed to make the essential calculations to calibrate their Eternity Device? If the Doctor could work that out, he could get there before them and be waiting.

'Track them down, rescue Gisella, thwart their plan, and defeat them,' the Doctor announced. 'Easy.' He clicked his fingers with satisfaction. 'Just like that.'

Every cloud has a silver lining.

Gisella had found a good hiding place. At least, she hoped she had. It was not as hard as she had feared to make her way round the ship. She had to avoid the Krashok troopers, but for the most part they seemed to be in their barracks or on the flight deck for the take-off.

Running repairs and more menial tasks were carried out by the service robots, which were now powered up and working again. There were plenty of those in evidence. But they were completely focused on their allocated tasks. Since they had been given no instructions about how to react to Gisella or to any stowaway, they simply ignored her.

She had wondered if she could give the robots orders of her own. Maybe get them to sabotage the ship, or even attack the Krashoks. But Gisella didn't think that would work. There would be overrides and fail-safes, and somewhere a Krashok monitoring the robots' network would see what was happening and know where she was and which robot she had tried to reprogramme.

So Gisella's best bet was to hide until the ship arrived somewhere. If she got a chance to get to the flight deck before they landed, then that would be a bonus. But probably she'd have to wait until the Krashoks disembarked somewhere. Then she could try to send a signal to the Doctor for help. Somehow.

Was he following? Would he find her? A part of

Gisella just wanted to hide and wait and hope he would come. But a part of her knew that she was on her own and if she was going to get lucky it would be because she made that luck herself.

For the moment she was safe, hiding at the back of a storage area behind a rack of shelves. The shelves were laden with various spare parts and components for the ship and even for the Krashoks themselves. From time to time service robots would come and get parts, ignoring Gisella if they saw her.

Soon, though, Gisella knew she might have to sneak out and see what was going on. There was a porthole in the outer wall above her head. By stacking several boxes and crates beneath it, Gisella had made a step up so she could get high enough to see out. Every time she checked, there was just the empty blackness of space, pin-pricked by stars and smudged with distant galaxies and nebulae.

From the other side of the door she could hear some sort of announcement. At the same time she detected a change in the tone of the engines. Were they slowing? Had they arrived? And if so – where?

Gisella stepped up on to the crates and peered out of the porthole. What she saw made her gasp with astonishment.

Hanging in space, right in front of them and growing rapidly larger as the Krashok ship approached, was an enormous brain.

Behind Gisella the door slid quietly open. Two armoured Krashoks stepped into the storage area.

Krashok Sergeant-at-Arms Jorak spoke in an electronically-enhanced voice. His words boomed round the room: 'We have an intruder on board!'

TARDIS

Data Bank

The Space Brain

Extract from 'The Mind Set — a case study in education techniques' by H. James Moore, University of Castillianus V, 2764

While the United Kingdom in the nineteenth, twentieth and twenty-first centuries on planet Earth offered an interesting case study into the education of children, it is another institution that is regarded as the best example of how to get the most from gifted and talented children.

In the UK, before the nineteenth century, there was very little formal education and very few schools. Most of the schools that did exist were run by the Church. But the Elementary Education Act of 1870 made it compulsory for children between the ages of five and ten to attend school. (Though in the countryside, children were often excused early if they were needed to work on farms.)

The minimum age for leaving school was raised to eleven in 1893, and to twelve in 1899. The leaving age was raised again to fourteen in 1918, with children expected to stay in education part time until they were eighteen. The minimum leaving age continued to rise – eventually to sixteen in 1973.

In the nineteenth century children from poorer families were allowed to leave school early and work to get money to help support the family if they had a certificate proving they had reached the required Educational Standard.

Similarly, the 'Universal Learning System' was set up by the Governors of Mygosuria. It ruled that the children of the Nine Galaxies should be educated to the highest standard no matter how old or young they were. There was no leaving age, and children were considered ready to move on to work or further study elsewhere when a computer assessment determined that they had reached their maximum potential.

As every child is different and learns in a different way, the teaching was tailored to the individual, and the level they were expected to achieve varied depending on their Ability Index which was worked out using the Hagen-Blotch method.

The most gifted children with the highest Ability Index were nicknamed The Mind Set, and they were sent to study at the famous Space Brain.

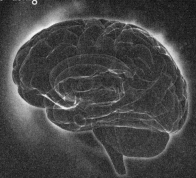

... Has a Silver Lining

It was clear from the TARDIS data banks, and from the Doctor's own memories of the era, that there was really only one place that the Krashoks could go. And it fit very neatly with the witch's words and prediction. They wouldn't want to risk a full attack, not before their precious Eternity Device was ready for action. Plus they would want the facilities they needed to use intact.

All of which pointed to a soft target – somewhere they could get access to the intelligence, knowledge and computing power they needed and that would not be heavily defended. So military installations and whole planets of learning were out.

'I know where you're going,' the Doctor chanted in a sing-song voice.

He set the controls, adjusted the co-ordinates, whacked the helmic regulator with his mallet, and was on his way.

The Doctor was going to find the brightest of the young. He was going to the Space Brain.

The Krashoks hadn't seen Gisella. She ducked down behind the shelves and kept as still and quiet as possible.

'We detected an unknown life form. It was traced to this area but we cannot get an exact location.'

'The ship is being searched now,' the second Krashok said to Sergeant-at-Arms Jorak. This Krashok had a massive claw at the end of one arm, and a spike protruding from the thumb on his other hand.

Like Sergeant Jorak, the other Krashok was an ugly mix of human, alien and robot. Both wore battle armour, grafted on to their patchwork bodies – bodies that brought together the most efficient and vicious pieces of other life forms they had conquered and killed.

A hard ruff of bony scales fanned out from behind both Krashoks necks – all Krashoks had these. Sergeant Jorak's ruff was hung with trophies of battle and insignias of rank. The other Krashok's ruff was less decorated – a few Killoran teeth on a cord, a space sheriff's badge taken from a recent kill and a lucky mega-rabbit's paw dangling on a thin metal chain.

'Make sure that all areas are searched,' Jorak insisted. 'Even storage areas like this. Who knows where the stowaway may be hiding.'

'Who indeed,' Gisella murmured. She risked a peep out over one of the shelves, and saw to her relief that the two Krashoks had turned back towards the door.

'The sensors detected alien life signs,' the second Krashok was saying. 'Though it is an odd reading – almost mechanical, but also sentient.' Its barbed tail whipped round as it turned.

'A cyborg perhaps,' Jorak said as he stepped out of the room. 'An organic-robot blend.'

The helmet grafted to his head swivelled as he surveyed the corridor outside. Gisella knew that the Krashok sergeant would be scanning all visual wavelengths including ultra violet and infra red as he searched for her.

'You're a fine one to talk about organic-robot blends,' she said quietly as the door closed behind them.

There was a metallic clang in the distance

that echoed round the ship. The floor shuddered beneath her. The Krashok ship had docked at the Space Brain, and it was time for Gisella to plan her escape.

The Doctor aimed the TARDIS at a quiet, unobtrusive point in the Space Brain. He wasn't sure exactly where it was, but from a plan of the structure he reckoned it should be pretty out of the way.

The TARDIS screen showed a schematic diagram of the whole of the Space Brain. It really did look just like a giant brain hanging in space.

'Wonder how it got its name?' the Doctor mused.

He opened the doors and stepped outside. Straight into a science lesson.

The pupils were all staring at the TARDIS – and now at the Doctor standing outside it. The teacher looked annoyed that he wasn't the focus of attention.

'Oh,' said the Doctor. 'Right. Hi,' he nodded and smiled and waved.

'That is so cool!' a girl exclaimed. 'We did teleportation techniques last week, before we all had to start on this special project thing, and it wasn't anything like as cool as that.'

'Thank you,' the Doctor said. Then he caught the teacher's eye. 'Er, carry on then, don't mind me.'

The teacher glared at the Doctor, looking like he was about to explode with anger.

'No need to behave any differently just because an Official Inspector from Of-Ed has turned up to observe how good the teaching is here on the Space Brain,' the Doctor assured them. He flashed his psychic paper so they could see how important he was. He made sure the seething teacher could see it clearly. 'No problem, I hope?'

'No problem at all,' the teacher said, switching on a smile. 'Can I be of any help?'

The Doctor grinned back at him. 'Oh yes.'

The Science teacher introduced himself as Professor Apricott, and seemed very happy to release two of the children from his class to give the Doctor a tour of the Space Brain.

'No problem at all,' he insisted. 'Everything, er, all right, is it?' He was rubbing his hands together hopefully, bushy eyebrows raised behind his thick-rimmed spectacles.

'Good so far,' the Doctor said. 'Can't give you the details, and I'll probably need to inspect some more later. But definitely heading in the right direction. On the right lines. Approaching from the onside part of the pitch. Promising,' he added, almost as an afterthought.

Professor Apricott forced a smile and picked out two of the children to take the Doctor on his tour. All the children put their hands up and shouted 'Me – me!'

The professor picked a boy and a girl. The girl was the one who thought the TARDIS arrival was so cool. She was called Caffey, and she had long fair hair and teeth that looked slightly too big for her mouth. The boy looked like a smaller version of Professor Apricott, with a shock of dark hair and thick-rimmed spectacles. His name was Kleb.

Caffey and Kleb were glad to be out of class for a bit, and seemed to enjoy showing the Doctor round. They looked in on Mr Tingle's Maths workshop, and an Art class where children were painting portraits of their teacher Ms Ferdinand. Algebra looked a bit boring, the Doctor thought, and he was sure that even Mr Louis was yawning as they sneaked in at the back for a few minutes. He couldn't understand why it was boring – they were studying space-dynamic contra-equations which were usually such fun.

In every classroom, the Doctor told them he was an Official Inspector and waved his psychic paper. In every classroom, he said: 'Don't mind me, just pretend I'm not here.' And in every classroom he just couldn't resist offering a teensy-weensy bit of advice.

In Algebra he mentioned the Colom-Smirnov way of reducing component parts, and Mr Louis gaped at him. In Space Geography, Miss Renfrew was astonished that the Doctor knew there was a planet called Doff, where because of a terrible mix-up with the computer that issued birth certificates everyone was called Clive. Even the girls. In Quantum Mechanics, the Doctor got glared at by Mrs Diffson for suggesting that there might be another parallel universe where Quantum Mechanics didn't work the same way.

'Of course,' he said to Caffey and Kleb as they left the lesson, 'there might even be another universe where Mrs Diffson has a sense of humour.' He paused and shook his head. 'Nah,' he decided. 'That's just too improbable.'

Gisella spent hours trying to get off the Krashok

ship. Every corridor she tried seemed to end at a wall or a room with no other exit. She tried exploring more dangerous areas where there were Krashok troopers patrolling.

She knew they were looking for her. The service robots had now been programmed to look out for unauthorized personnel on board, so every time Gisella stepped from the shadows or emerged from hiding she was taking a big risk.

Finally, she found herself in a small sub-control room. There was a scanner screen linked up to the security systems, and Gisella discovered she could tune it into the optical circuits of some of the Krashok troopers. She could see what they saw – the images relayed from their cybernetic eye-implants to the network, and appearing on Gisella's screen.

But for the most part that was pretty boring and unhelpful. More useful was a schematic map of the section of the ship she was in. Marked clearly on the map was the main airlock exit. If Gisella could get there, she could escape from the ship. Small symbols also marked the position of every Krashok and service robot. There were so many of them, Gisella realized, it would be hard to get past them and escape.

The problem was finding a safe route that was as short as possible. She set the computer to calculate the best route, avoiding the Krashoks and service robots.

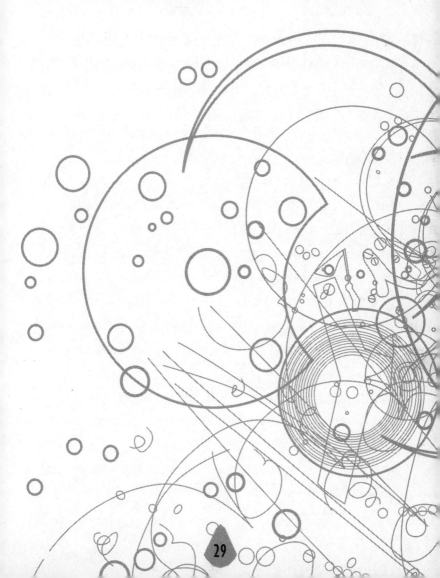

Activity

You are currently in Sub-Control 3. Calculate a route to Main Exit Airlock avoiding all Krashoks and Service Robots...

Sub-Control 3

Main Exit Airlock

With the route worked out and memorized, Gisella stepped out into the service corridor outside the small control room. Right into the path of an approaching Krashok.

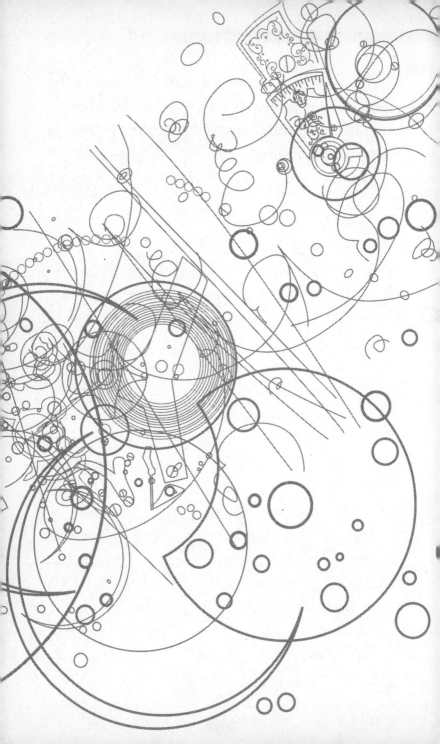

Escape to Danger

Gisella skidded to a halt. She turned to run the other way. But there was a Krashok approaching from the other direction too. It raised its arm, a powerful blaster built into the stump of its wrist where the hand should be.

Gisella gave a shriek of surprise and hurled herself back into the sub-control room. She thumped the door control and the door slid smoothly closed behind her. Quickly, Gisella took off one of her shoes, and slammed the heel of it into the controls. There was a spray of sparks.

From the other side of the door, she could hear the Krashoks trying to get in. There was a thump, and a dent appeared in the metal of the door. It wouldn't keep them out for long.

And there was no other way out. Gisella was trapped.

The monitor screen was still displaying the map

of this section of the ship, showing the route to the main airlock. But that was useless now.

Gisella worked frantically at the controls, calling up more detailed schematics and plans of the area she was in. She was looking for a way out. Maybe there was a ventilation shaft, or a wiring conduit – any way she could get out of this small room before the Krashoks broke through the door.

The hammering from the door was becoming louder and more insistent. There must be several Krashoks out there now. The metal was like the cratered surface of the Moon, it was so dented and misshapen. They would be through any minute.

Finally she found what she was looking for. There was a service panel on the side wall that could be removed to allow access to the wires and pipes behind. The panel on the other side of the wall could be opened too, allowing access to the same wires and pipes from the next room. If Gisella could get the panels off, she could climb through and slip away down the corridor while the Krashoks were busy breaking into this room. Maybe.

It was a big *maybe*, and she would have to work quickly. Gisella switched off the monitor screen so it wouldn't give any clues to where she had gone. Then she hurried to the access panel. If she didn't know it was there, she would never have found it. The only clue that it could be removed was a tiny indentation at one side where it could be pressed.

Just pressing at the right point operated a mechanism and the panel sprung open. Behind it was a mass of wires and tubes. Gisella pushed inside, pulling the panel closed behind her. She fumbled in the dark for the panel on the other side, easing her way through the maze of wires and tubes, hoping she didn't break any. If she did, she might be sprayed with acid or scalding water from a tube, or frazzled by an electric shock from a wire.

For a while she thought she was trapped inside the wall. The panel behind her had clicked shut, and there didn't seem to be any way of opening it again – or of opening the panel on the other side so she could escape.

She could hear the muffled hammering of the Krashoks as they tried to break into the control room she had just left. Then a terrific crash as the door was smashed open.

At the same moment, Gisella's fingers finally found the release catch on the access panel. The metal plate swung open and she tumbled through into the room beyond. Gisella leaped to her feet, ready to run.

But right in front of her was Sergeant Jorak. The ring of scales protruding from his neck quivered with satisfaction.

'How very predictable,' Jorak rasped.

Behind him, several more Krashoks stepped into the room. They advanced on Gisella.

'Take her to Commander Grelt,' Jorak said.

Gisella felt very small, standing in front of the huge, impressive figure of Commander Grelt.

The Krashok leader walked slowly round her, as if to check Gisella really was that small. His yellowing tusks were frighteningly close to Gisella's face. Then abruptly, Grelt turned to Sergeant Jorak.

'You have done well, *Acting Commander* Jorak.'

Jorak snapped to attention. 'Thank you, sir.'

'Your battlefield promotion will be confirmed by Krashok Command as soon as we break communications silence to report our mission has been accomplished.' Grelt nodded with satisfaction. 'With two commanders again we are once more up to full strength.'

The other Krashoks saluted and gave a brief

cheer: 'Ha!'

Gisella was trying her best not to show how frightened she was. But even so, she shrank away as Grelt approached her again.

'You were in the warehouse, with the Darksmiths. So, perhaps you are responsible for the death of Commander Skraar.'

He rested a clawed hand on Gisella's shoulder, turning her so she was forced to look up at him. But what Grelt said next frightened her more than anything:

'Search her.'

Two Krashoks took hold of Gisella's arms, stretching them out while a third patted her down and checked her pockets.

'What is this?' the Krashok wondered as it pulled something from Gisella's pocket.

The creature held up what it had found, holding its egg-sized prize surprisingly delicately between two vicious-looking claws.

It was the Eternity Crystal. Not the copy that the Doctor and Gisella had been given by Varlos – she had already managed to swap that for the real one. And now the Krashoks had found the real Eternity Crystal.

'It must be a fake, a duplicate copy,' Acting Commander Jorak announced. 'We should destroy it.'

For a moment, Gisella felt elated. She struggled to hide her feelings, not wanting the Krashoks to realize the truth – that this was in fact the real Crystal.

But then Commander Grelt said: 'No. She was with the Darksmiths. She may already have replaced the real Crystal with a copy. We must analyze them both and find out which is real and which is a fake.'

Grelt leaned close to Gisella. 'Whichever it is,' he said quietly, 'your ruse has failed. And as soon as we have used our mind probe analyzers to extract every gramme of knowledge from your brain, you will be executed.'

Despite the dedication of the teachers and the enthusiasm of the pupils that he had seen, the Doctor had to admit that the whole place was a bit the worse for wear. There was paint peeling from walls and ceilings. There was dust – even cobwebs – in the corners.

'I don't like to say it,' the Doctor told his two young guides, 'but the Space Brain is looking a bit run down.'

Ceffey nodded. 'It's the funding,' she explained.

'*Lack of* funding,' Kleb said. 'Everyone agrees this place is really important, but no one wants to pay for it. We got some space-lottery grants last year which helped.'

'Even so,' Caffey added, 'they ask our parents to make a contribution every term to the Brain-Fund. And we had to pay for our class trip to the Findolonus Museum of Windows.'

The Doctor was almost speechless with surprise. 'You mean to tell me,' he said, 'that there's a museum of *windows*?'

'Not *just* windows,' Kleb assured him enthusiastically. 'They've got some doors too.'

'There's a big special exhibition at the moment, that's why we went,' Caffey explained.

'About the Defenestration of Prague,' Kleb added.

'Oh,' the Doctor said. 'So broken windows, too.'

'These three blokes got thrown out of a window,' Kleb said. 'In Prague. In 1618.'

The Doctor nodded. 'I remember.'

'They survived because they landed on a pile of manure,' Kleb went on. Caffey rolled her eyes.

The Doctor nodded. 'I know. Who do you

think put it there. The TARDIS stank for a week.'

He shook his head sadly. 'A museum of *windows*?!' He sighed, then clapped his hands together. 'Right then, I think I've seen everything I need to.'

'You're finished?' Caffey asked.

'Oh yes.'

'You're leaving?' Kleb asked.

'Oh no. Just need to see the Principal, or Head Teacher or whatever he's called and make my report.'

'Mr Skillmore's office is just along here.' Kleb glanced nervously at Caffey. 'Do you need us there as well or can we go back to class? We've got this special project we're supposed to be working on...'

'Oh no, you come with me. I want to say how helpful you've been. Maybe you'll get a gold star or a sticker or a badge or a certificate or something.'

'Hey, cool!' Caffey decided.

The Principal's door was made of panelled wood. There was a small plaque on it that read: 'Principal August Skillmore'. The Doctor smiled reassuringly at Caffey and Kleb, then knocked on the door.

The voice that answered was loud and clear and full of authority: 'Enter.'

'You see,' the Doctor said. 'Nothing to worry about.'

He opened the door and they went through. The Principal's office was lined with bookcases and dominated by a large desk. Behind the desk was a huge window looking out into space. A figure was sitting behind the desk, and rose to its feet as the Doctor and his friends entered.

Through the window, the Doctor could see the stark, brutal shape of the Krashok warship, attached to an airlock door at the side of the office by a transparent tube.

The figure rising to its feet on the other side of the desk raised an arm that was encased in a series of tubes – a Glasterion Multi-Fire Blaster Array. The other arm was the savagely clawed foreleg of a Renevian tiger. The figure behind the desk was a Krashok.

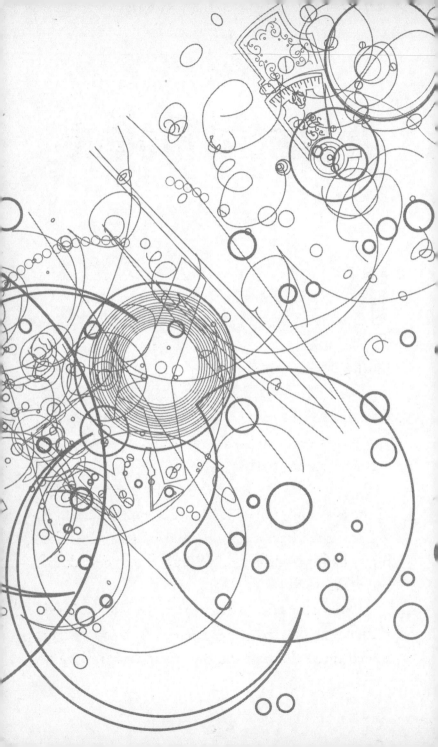

A Special Project

'**W**hat is that?' Caffey demanded.

'It's not Principal Skillmore,' Kleb said.

'It certainly isn't,' the Doctor said. He walked slowly towards the desk, his hands held up in surrender.

When he reached the desk, the Doctor leaned forward. 'Hello there!' He lowered his hands, and rested them on the edge of the desk. Or that was what he seemed to be doing.

But then the Doctor suddenly grabbed the edge of the desk and heaved it up and over. The Krashok was knocked backwards. It fired its guns, but the blasts hammered harmlessly into the underside of the desk.

The Doctor was already running. He grabbed Caffey with one hand and Kleb with the other and pulled them through the door before slamming it shut behind them.

'Krashok!' the Doctor explained. He aimed his sonic screwdriver at the lock.

'What's a Krashok?' Caffey asked.

'How did it get here?' Kleb wanted to know. 'And where's Principal Skillmore?'

'Dead, I expect,' the Doctor said. 'Sorry.'

'What do we do now?' Kleb asked.

The door exploded into splinters of smouldering wood.

'Run!' the Doctor yelled.

They raced down the corridor, not daring to look and see if the Krashok was coming after them.

'Where are we going?' Kleb gasped.

'You tell me,' the Doctor said. He slowed to a walk. 'I don't think they're following.'

'They?' Caffey said. 'I only saw one.'

'There are a lot more than that,' the Doctor said. 'I was hoping I'd got here before them, obviously I was wrong.'

'You knew they were coming here?' Kleb asked.

The Doctor nodded. 'Hoped they were.'

'Hoped?!' Caffey was amazed.

But the Doctor grinned. 'Oh yes. You see, my friend Gisella is trapped on their ship. So while I'm not too chuffed they're out to kill me, I'm glad I found them, because now I can rescue her.'

'But why here?' Kleb wondered. 'What are they after?'

'They're after your minds,' the Doctor said. 'Your intelligence and ability. You mentioned a special project – I'll bet that's something the Krashoks have set up.'

'We don't know much about it,' Kleb admitted. 'But we got a load of new equipment for the science labs. Computational arrays and multi-platform sequencing processors. Serious stuff.'

'Boring stuff,' Caffey put in. 'But the teachers gave us all work programmes we had to do on the new equipment. Problem solving, and calculations. It was quite hard – even for Kleb and he's a whizz at maths and stuff.'

Kleb smiled at the compliment. 'So what's it all about, Doctor?'

'The Krashoks need some difficult calculations done in a hurry,' the Doctor explained. 'They have a device that will make sure they win any battle they fight.'

'Cool,' Caffey said.

The Doctor shook his head. 'No. Not cool at

all. It will bring their dead and injured back to life and restore them to full health. It'll make them invincible. And believe me, that's not a good thing. They're a nasty vicious lot, the Krashoks. As you just saw.'

From somewhere behind them came the sound of an explosion.

'We believe you,' Caffey said quickly.

'Krashoks?' Kleb asked.

The Doctor nodded. 'They've realized they've been rumbled. Now they're coming to make sure they get the answers to those calculations.'

'And what are we going to do?' Caffey asked.

'We're going to warn the staff and the pupils. And we're going to rescue Gisella. And we're going to stop them.'

There were several teachers in the staff room on breaks between their lessons. One of them the Doctor recognized as Miss Renfrew from Space Geography. He hurried over, flashing his psychic paper again.

'Of-Ed Defensive Department,' he said. 'Sorry not to warn you earlier, but there are dangerous aliens docked to the Space Brain. They've already killed Principal Skillmore, and they're about to attack. Sorry about that.'

The staff stared at him in disbelief. Miss Renfrew laughed nervously.

'It's true,' Caffey insisted. 'We were nearly killed by a Krashok.'

'A what?' Miss Renfrew said. 'Really, I think this joke has gone quite far enough.'

There was the distant sound of an explosion. The Doctor went and opened the door wide. Another explosion roared through the Space Brain.

'Does it sound like I'm joking?' he demanded.

'It's the special project,' Kleb said. 'They did some sort of deal with the Principal for the new equipment. Then they killed him. They're after the answers to the problems they set us. That's what they need.'

'I don't believe there is any such thing as a Krashok,' Miss Renfrew said.

But one of the other teachers was shaking his head. He was a tall, elderly man with thinning white hair. 'The Krashoks are a nasty lot, I'm afraid,' he said. 'Militaristic and acquisitive. Augment themselves with bits and pieces from all sorts of other races. Weapons mainly. If Inspector…'

'Doctor,' the Doctor corrected.

'If Doctor, er…'

'Just the Doctor.'

'If the Doctor is right, we are in big trouble.' He reached out to shake the Doctor's hand. 'I'm Mr Gershwinn, Head of the Alien Life Form Department. Pleased to meet you.'

'Alien Life Forms?' The Doctor grinned. 'You're head of a department called ALF.'

'That's me,' the man agreed. 'Alf Gershwinn.' He smiled. 'Fits very nicely, don't you think?'

'Oh yes. It's brilliant.'

'Well, assuming this Doctor is right…' one of the other teachers said, peering at the Doctor over her horn-rimmed spectacles. The room shook under the force of another explosion. '…And it sounds as if he is – then what can we do about it?'

'I want you to get yourselves to the best room you can defend. Somewhere big enough for all the children and staff. Lock yourselves in, barricade the doors. Lock down any shutters or seals you can – anything to slow down the Krashoks. And most of all, destroy the equipment in the science labs and stop the calculations.'

'The main Assembly Hall is probably the best place to get everyone,' the woman said. The other staff nodded in agreement.

'I'll send an e-message to all the classrooms. It will flash up on their whiteboards,' Mr Gershwinn said.

'And the science labs are on the way from here,' Miss Renfrew added. 'We'll do what we can on the way.' She turned to Caffey and Kleb. 'I think you two had better come with us.'

'No way,' Caffey said. 'We're going with the Doctor.'

'He needs to rescue his friend,' Kleb explained. 'Isn't that right, Doctor?'

But there was no answer. The Doctor had gone.

The Krashoks were moving through the Space Brain in an orderly manner. They stopped at every door, checking the room beyond was clear. If they weren't sure, or if there was anything inside they thought could be used as a weapon against them, they threw in explosive grenades and blew up the room.

It was a systematic and thorough operation. But the Doctor only had to watch them for a minute before he worked out that the routine they were following so exactly was also a weakness.

There was a gap of several seconds when the Krashok troopers went into rooms either side of the main corridor, when that same corridor was left empty. During that time, the Doctor sprinted past the Krashoks. Once behind their lines, he made his way back to the Principal's office.

He knew that there would be other Krashoks following up, and he proceeded cautiously. Several times he had to duck into a devastated room to hide as more Krashoks advanced down into the Space Brain. But because they knew the advance guard had already checked all the rooms, they didn't see any reason to check them again.

'No imagination,' the Doctor said sadly. 'Mind you, that could be part of the problem. If only you lot had stayed at home telling each other stories and singing about heroes and monsters and damsels rescuing dragons in distress then you wouldn't need to go charging about other people's schools and getting the Darksmiths to invent terrible weapons of mass un-destruction.'

Soon he was back at the Principal's office. The Doctor crept through the ruined doorway. The airlock door was open, leading into the transparent tube that snaked across to the Krashok ship.

'Hope no one's watching,' the Doctor murmured as he started across.

The view from the tube was magnificent. But the Doctor was distracted from the beautiful view of the stars and nebulae by the sight of the Space Brain. It really did look like a giant brain, but with tiny windows round the edges. He shook his head sadly as he saw explosions light up several of the windows.

He needed to find Gisella fast so he could get back and help. But for the moment, Gisella was more important – because she had the real Eternity Crystal and whatever else happened, the Krashoks mustn't get hold of it. And because she was his friend.

The airlock door at the other end of the tube hissed open when the Doctor applied his sonic screwdriver to the coded lock. Once through he had no idea where he was going. The ship was plain and functional. Like he'd said – no imagination.

But there was an information terminal close by, fixed to the wall. The Doctor managed to find a schematic map of the ship, and located the cell block. That would be where the Krashoks kept their prisoners. The Doctor hoped they hadn't found Gisella, but if they had he needed to get to her quickly.

And if they hadn't, then it was as good a place to start as any.

He managed to avoid meeting any more Krashoks. Most of them must now be over in the Space Brain. But there were service robots everywhere. They might have been programmed to look out for intruders, or they might not care. The Doctor didn't know, but he wasn't going to take any chances.

A quick adjustment to the sonic screwdriver, and he set it to emit a high-pitched sound wave. The sound interfered with the robots' optical systems – making them blind as he approached. The robots froze, running diagnostic programmes to try to work out what the problem was. They only started to move again once the Doctor had moved out of range – and out of sight.

Eventually, he found himself at the door to the cell block. He took a deep breath and opened the door. Ahead of him was a line of heavy metal doors with barred windows. Through the first of these the

Doctor saw an empty, plain, metal room equipped with just a low bed.

But when he saw into the second room, he gasped in sudden fury.

Gisella was lying on the bed. Beside her, a bank of hi-tech equipment had been wheeled into place. A mass of tubes and wires connected the equipment to Gisella's head.

As the Doctor opened the door, Gisella's eyes opened.

'Help me, Doctor,' she said. 'They're taking my mind!'

He stared at the wires and tubes, and examined the equipment. 'I'm sorry,' he said at last. 'It's a sophisticated mind probe device, and I'm not sure that I can disconnect it without emptying your brain completely.'

'You have to try.'

'But if I get it wrong – it'll kill you!'

The Eternity Chamber

'**D**on't get it wrong, then,' Gisella said. She smiled bravely through the mass of wires and tubes.

The Doctor examined the equipment again. He traced wires with his fingers, and studied where tubes went. He whirred his sonic screwdriver over the whole apparatus and checked the readings on a small screen set into the bank of equipment.

'Right,' he announced at last. 'I have to disconnect all type T tubes first, unless they are connected to neutral-loaded wires. I need to disconnect the neutral-loaded wires next, and then any of the type T tubes that are remaining. After that I can switch off the power, then unplug any positive-loaded wires and then the rest of the tubes. Finally, I can detach the rest of the wires.'

'Go on then,' Gisella said nervously. 'What are you waiting for?'

The Doctor had managed to display a diagram on the screen. It showed all the wires and tubes, with their types marked. He took a felt pen from his pocket and tapped it against the screen.

'I think I'll work out the order here first, before I try anything,' he said.

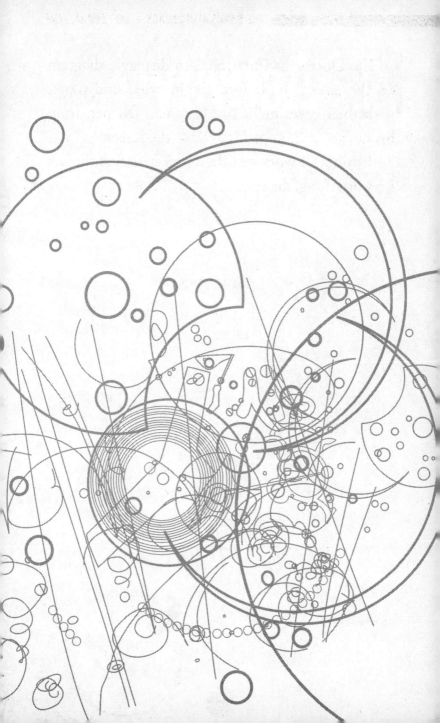

Activity

EQUIPMENT

KEY

Type 'T' Tube	Positive Wire
Other (not T) Tubes	Neutral Wire
	Negative Wire

POWER
SUPPLY

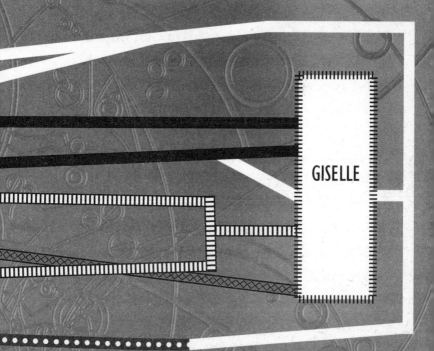

GISELLE

Mark the order in which to detach and disconnect tubes,
wires, and power supply without harming Gisella.

Gisella lay very still, aware that the machinery was draining her memories from her. But as the Doctor disconnected the systems, she felt everything come flooding back.

'I've put you back as you were,' the Doctor said. 'Luckily the Krashoks didn't seem to realize you have a robotic brain in there not an organic one. I just uploaded everything again, and you're as good as new.'

He disconnected the positive-loaded wire, then ripped out the rest of the tubes. Finally, he pulled off the last wires, and helped Gisella to her feet.

'How are you feeling?'

'Not quite as good as new,' she said. 'But not too wobbly. Thank goodness you found me.'

'Just in time,' the Doctor agreed. 'Now tell me – did the Krashoks find the Eternity Crystal?'

Gisella looked away embarrassed and ashamed. 'Yes, they did. I'm sorry.'

The Doctor pulled her into a hug. 'Not you fault. You're all right, that's all that matters. And now we're free on the Krashok ship without them knowing, we can sabotage their Eternity Device anyway. No problem.'

'Simple as that?' Gisella asked, laughing despite herself.

'Well,' the Doctor said. 'Maybe not *that* simple.' He pointed to the screen, which was still displaying the diagram of tubes and wires and his felt tip labels showing the order in which to remove them. 'Got to be easier than sorting out this lot though. Don't you think?'

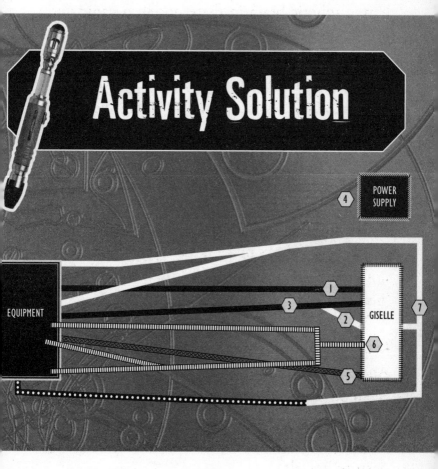

Activity Solution

POWER SUPPLY ④

EQUIPMENT

① ③ ② GISELLE ⑦ ⑥ ⑤

The Doctor and Gisella crept along the corridor which the Doctor knew from studying the layout of the ship led to where they wanted to go. There were fewer service robots in this part of the Krashok ship, but the Doctor had the sonic screwdriver set to confuse their visual circuits anyway.

'It feels like we're getting deeper into the Krashok domain,' Gisella whispered.

The lighting had slowly changed from harsh white to a bloodstained red. The shadows seemed to deepen the further they went. The air seemed heavy, and the corridor echoed with an increasing hum of power.

'I think we're getting close,' the Doctor said.

'But close to what?' Gisella asked.

In answer, the Doctor paused in front of a large doorway. He adjusted the sonic screwdriver, and its pitch changed. The end glowed blue, and the door slid quietly open.

'The Eternity Chamber,' the Doctor said.

The room beyond was even darker. It was so large Gisella couldn't see to the far side. But her attention was focused on the huge device in the centre of the room. It was a massive piece of equipment. Cables hung round the edges. Coils and tubes were lit from within. Wires connected different components. And right in the heart of the device the Eternity Crystal throbbed with inner light and power.

'Is that the real Crystal?' Gisella asked. 'Have they replaced the fake?'

The Doctor nodded. 'Looks like it's powering up. The fake Crystal wouldn't be able to absorb the power like that. See how it glows that bright blue? It's the crystalline matrix that Varlos devised that does that as it stores and boosts the power.' The Doctor smiled. 'There is another way I can tell, actually.'

'What's that?'

'They chucked away the fake Crystal when they'd worked out which was the real one.' The Doctor bent down and picked up an identical Crystal from the floor close by. Except this Crystal wasn't glowing. 'Here it is, you see. Busted. Lost its gleam.' He slipped it into his pocket. 'Oh well, it was a good try.'

'Can't we sabotage the device?' Gisella asked. 'Dismantle it?'

'Not while it's powered up like this. They must be testing the systems. If they power it down, we could swap the Crystals again and they'd never know until they use it. But for the moment, there's nothing we can do.'

'So they're ready to activate the device now,' Gisella realized. 'We're too late. We've failed.'

'Not yet, we haven't. As soon as they have the calculations complete they can calibrate it to work only on Krashoks. They'll have to power down to do that, of course. Then they'll start the countdown. But if we can make sure the calculations are never completed...'

'How do we do that?'

'Help the staff and students on the Space Brain to fight off the Krashoks and dismantle their equipment there.'

'So what are we waiting for?'

The Doctor raised his eyebrows. 'You're the one asking all the questions and slowing us down.'

Gisella glared at him. But she knew the Doctor was only teasing. 'Come on then,' she said. 'Slow coach.'

Together they left the Eternity Chamber and hurried back through the Krashok ship. They were almost back at the airlock when they rounded a corner, and came face to face with a service robot.

The robot stared at them, eyes glowing a fierce red. 'Intruders!' it barked in its metallic voice.

The Doctor raised the sonic screwdriver. The robot staggered back.

'Visual circuits damaged,' it complained. It blundered back and forth across the corridor, and the Doctor and Gisella dodged past it.

'That was a narrow escape,' Gisella said, looking back at the confused robot.

'Narrow, yes,' the Doctor agreed. 'But not so much of an escape.'

Gisella whirled round. Ahead of them, advancing menacingly down the corridor, were three Krashok troopers. They raised their weapons and prepared to fire.

Fighting Back

The Doctor and Gisella turned to run. But two more Krashoks had appeared at the other end of the corridor.

'Doctor – we're trapped,' Gisella realized.

They both ducked as the wall beside them exploded. Energy bolts flew down the corridor. The Doctor and Gisella dodged and ran. But they were being driven away from the airlock exit and towards the approaching Krashoks.

Then suddenly there was an explosion from *behind* the attacking Krashoks, and the corridor started to fill with smoke. A black cloud rolled over the Krashoks, heading for the Doctor and Gisella.

'What caused that?' Gisella gasped.

'No idea,' the Doctor admitted. 'Bit of luck, though.'

They dived into the smoke. The Doctor had hold

of Gisella's hand. With his other hand he felt along the corridor wall. The dark shape of a Krashok trooper loomed out of the fog for a moment. Then it was gone.

Soon the Doctor and Gisella were emerging from the other side of the smoke into clear air. They tried not to cough, knowing that would alert the Krashoks to where they were.

From inside the rolling ball of smoke came the sound of blaster fire and a body slumping to the floor.

'They can't see what they're doing,' the Doctor said quietly. 'They're shooting each other.'

'What do we do now?'

The Doctor was looking down the corridor away from the smoke, towards the airlock. 'We get out of here,' he told her. 'And we've got a few thank yous to say as well.'

In the airlock doorway, Gisella could see two small figures peering out into the corridor. There was a boy with dark-rimmed glasses, and a girl with long blond hair. They were grinning and waving.

The Doctor and Gisella ran to the airlock.

'Quickly,' the boy said. 'The smoke will

clear soon. It's only a mix of hydrocarbons in colloidal suspension. Harmless but thick. Only it disperses very quickly when the surface tension breaks down.'

'Kleb made it in the Chemistry lab,' the girl said proudly.

The Doctor ushered them all through the airlock and down the transparent tube that led across to the Space Brain. As they hurried through the tube, he introduced Gisella to Kleb and the girl, Caffey.

'Glad the Doctor managed to rescue you,' Caffey said.

'Oh, he's always doing that,' Gisella told her. 'He's getting quite good at it.'

'Oh cheers,' the Doctor said. 'Let's do marks out of ten for the rescue effort later when we're safe, shall we?'

'Aren't we safe when we get back to the Space Brain?' Gisella asked.

'There are Krashoks everywhere,' Kleb said. 'We were lucky to be able to sneak into the Chemistry lab. But the Physics block is off-limits.'

'Is that where the Krashok equipment is?' the Doctor asked.

'Afraid so,' Caffey told him. 'Miss Renfrew and

Mr Gershwinn tried to get in, but the whole area is sealed off and guarded by these Krashok things.'

'Bad news?' Gisella guessed.

The Doctor nodded. They had reached the other end of the tube and emerged cautiously into the Principal's office on the Space Brain.

'OK, silent running,' the Doctor said. 'That means we need to run, and we do it silently. Got that?'

Everyone nodded.

'Where are we going?' Gisella whispered.

'Everyone else has gone to the Assembly Hall, like the Doctor said,' Caffey told them.

'Right then, that's where you lot are headed,' the Doctor decided.

'What about you?' Gisella asked.

'I'll see if I can get to the Physics lab and stop the Krashoks from finishing their calculations.'

'Then I'm coming with you,' Gisella told him.

'We all are,' Kleb said, and Caffey nodded her head in agreement.

The Doctor sighed. 'No, you're not. I need you to keep the Krashoks busy. Cause trouble, so they have to send troopers away from the lab and then maybe I can get in.'

'If they're using the main computer systems,' Kleb said, 'we might be able to hack in and stop them anyway. There are fibre optic network links running under the Assembly Hall floor.'

'Good idea,' the Doctor said. He grinned. 'So that's a plan then. You try to draw the Krashoks away from the lab, and hack into their systems. I'll see if I can sabotage their equipment so they never complete their calculations.'

Gisella folded her arms and fixed the Doctor with a stare. 'And if that doesn't work?'

He shrugged. 'Plan B. Whatever that is.'

Gisella didn't like to leave the Doctor on his own. But she knew he was right – Caffey and Kleb and the others on the Space Brain needed her help. The Doctor, of course, could look after himself.

Kleb had one more of the smoke bombs he'd made, which they decided to use to get past the slowly advancing Krashoks between them and the Assembly Hall.

'Mr Gershwinn and Professor Apricott were talking about setting booby traps for the Krashoks,'

Caffey said.

'Then let's be careful we don't set them off,' Gisella told her. 'Any idea what they had planned?'

'They didn't say,' Kleb told her.

Soon they could hear the Krashoks moving ahead of them, clearing rooms and advancing down corridors. The dull crump of explosions echoed through the Space Brain.

Gisella, Caffey and Kleb crept along the corridor. They peered round a corner, and saw the line of advancing Krashoks in front of them.

'They're taking their time,' Caffey said quietly.

'No hurry,' Kleb pointed out. 'They just want to keep everyone away from the labs where they've got their equipment working.'

'Time to start causing trouble so they send more troopers,' Gisella said. 'You got that smoke bomb ready?'

Kleb nodded. He produced a glass test tube from his pocket. It was filled with a yellow liquid, and sealed with a rubber cork at the top.

'Is that it?'

'Sure is.'

'Way cool,' Caffey murmured. 'So go on – chuck it at them!'

They crept closer to the Krashoks, keeping as quiet as possible. But not quiet enough. One of the Krashoks turned slowly towards them. Its metal-clad face twisted into what might have been a smile. It raised its arm, a Megalanian Machine Pistol was braced to his forearm. The muzzle glowed as the weapon powered up ready to fire.

'Now!' Gisella shouted.

The other Krashoks started to turn too – just as Kleb hurled the test tube at them. Gisella pushed Kleb and Caffey aside and dived for cover herself as blaster fire ripped down the corridor. The floor where they had just been standing exploded in flames. Then the corridor filled rapidly with dark smoke.

'Come on!' Gisella told the others.

Together, they ran into the smoke. The Krashoks were dark silhouettes in the cloudy air. Gisella pushed past. She was vaguely aware of Kleb and Caffey close to her.

Suddenly, she was out the other side. Kleb ran through beside her, and paused, gasping for breath.

He grinned. 'We made it.' But then his smile faded. 'Where's Caffey?'

They both turned back towards the rolling smoke. The muffled sound of gunfire came from within. There was a scream. Then silence.

The corridors leading to the main Physics lab were guarded by Krashoks – one at each junction. There would be more in the lab itself, the Doctor guessed. They were desperate to make sure their equipment finished the calculations the gifted pupils and their brilliant teachers had been tricked into programming into the computers.

The Doctor ducked back into cover as a Krashok turned towards him. After a while, he peeped round the corner of the corridor again, and was relieved to see the Krashok had resumed its pacing up and down across the corridor junction. It hadn't seen him.

But how could he get past? How long did he have until the calculations were complete? How soon would Gisella and her friends cause a distraction – and would it be soon enough?

As he watched, another Krashok appeared from a doorway further down the corridor. It ran to the patrolling Krashok, and spoke urgently:

'The Advance Clearance Force is under attack.

Commander Grelt has ordered us to reinforce them and offer support.'

The other Krashok nodded. 'Good. I could do with some action, rather than standing around here.'

The Doctor quickly found a room to hide in as the two Krashoks ran past him. He waited a minute, and sure enough, several more Krashoks followed. The diversion must be working.

The corridor to the labs seemed clear now. But the Doctor remained cautious. He picked his way warily along the corridor, and breathed a sigh of relief when he reached the main doors. A sign said: 'Physics 1 – Main Laboratory'. This must be it.

Would there be more Krashoks on guard inside? There was only one way to find out. The Doctor opened the door and slipped inside.

One whole side of the large room was taken up with the Krashok equipment. It was whirring and bleeping happily as it did its job. Lights flashed and needles quivered on dials. A large screen displayed the message:

Time to Completion – 3:42

As the Doctor watched, the forty-two became forty-one, became forty, became thirty-nine. He couldn't afford to wait any longer. He took out his sonic screwdriver and ran for the equipment. He had to stop it now.

He was almost at the equipment when a large Krashok trooper stepped out from behind it. He raised a power-blaster. The Doctor could hear the weapon charging up ready to fire, and skidded to a halt.

'Oh, hi there,' the Doctor said. 'Don't shoot. I'm looking for Commander Grelt. He asked me to check the polarity of the neutron flow.' The Doctor brandished his sonic screwdriver. 'So, if you could just let me at the machinery, this won't take a minute.'

The Krashok didn't look convinced. But at least it hadn't fired its gun.

'It's OK,' the Doctor said soothingly. 'Just ask Commander Grelt.'

Behind him, the door slammed shut. The Doctor whirled round – to see another Krashok standing behind him. Its neck-ruff was hanging with trophies and the insignia of a commander. Yellow tusks jutted out from its slavering mouth.

'Ask me what, Doctor?' Commander Grelt demanded.

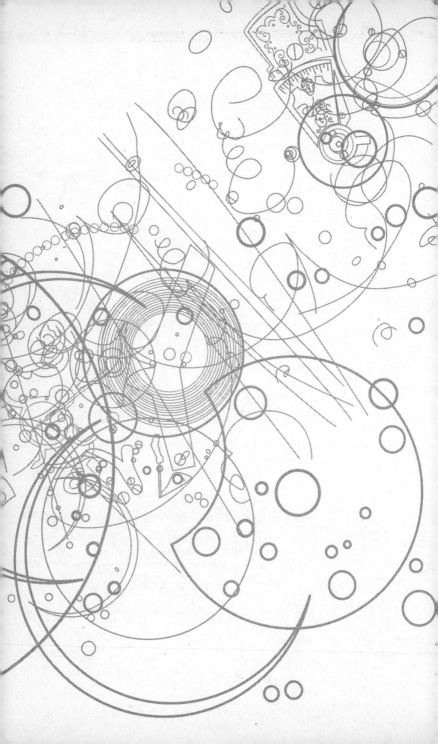

Failure?

From inside the smoke, Gisella could hear the sound of shouted orders, confused cries and the noise of gunfire. There had been just one scream from Caffey, then silence.

'I'm sorry,' Gisella said to Kleb. 'We can't wait any longer.'

'I know.' Kleb wiped his eyes. 'The smoke will clear any moment now.'

His eyes widened, and Gisella turned to see what he was looking at. She expected a Krashok to emerge from the smoke, blaster ready to fire. But instead it was a girl with long fair hair and a sooty face.

'Caffey!' Kleb exclaimed. He ran to hug her.

'Oi – get off!' Caffey pulled herself free. 'I thought we were in a hurry,' she complained.

'We are,' Gisella agreed. 'But we thought... We heard you scream.'

'I didn't scream,' Caffey insisted. She looked away. 'I just sort of yelled.'

'It sounded like a scream,' Kleb told her, suppressing a grin.

'Well it wasn't. I *don't* scream – all right? Now, let's get out of here. There are loads more Krashoks arriving, and that smoke is beginning to clear.'

'Reckon we've got the Doctor that diversion he wanted then,' Kleb said as they hurried off towards the Assembly Hall.

'Let's hope it worked,' Gisella said.

The Doctor was held between two huge Krashok troopers. Commander Grelt walked slowly all round him.

'Such a small man,' he said. 'Did you really think you could defeat the Krashoks, Doctor?'

The Doctor made a show of considering before he replied. 'Not really. I suppose not. Doubt it. Well, you never know. No harm in trying.'

'And you are very trying.' Grelt looked round the assembled Krashoks to check they were suitably amused.

'Oh yeah,' the Doctor said. 'Good one. Like it. So...' He nodded at the equipment in front of them. 'This would be calculating the right calibration matrix for the Eternity Device would it?'

Grelt halted abruptly. He turned slowly to glare at the Doctor. 'What do you know of that?'

'Oh, I looked after the Eternity Crystal for a while. Borrowed it from the Darksmith Collective. Even visited Karagula to see how they were getting along. Lovely planet. Bit dark indoors, but lovely, don't you think?' He sighed and nodded as if remembering. 'But of course, you met on Ursulonamex, didn't you. The Planet of Oblivion. Lots of oblivion there now.' His voice hardened. 'But you'd know all about that, wouldn't you?'

'I was going to have you executed,' Grelt said. 'But now I have a better idea.' Saliva dripped off the end of one of his tusks and splashed on the Doctor's shoe.

'Oh,' he complained. 'New trainers,' he admonished. 'Well, nearly new. Jumble sale. Or maybe a car boot, I don't remember. So – no execution then?'

'Instead you will watch the completion of our victory.' Grelt turned to point at the equipment behind. The countdown on the screen reached zero.

There was a reassuring 'ping' from the machinery.

The Doctor sniffed. 'Was that it? Very impressive. So, can I be executed now? I mean, it's got to be better than listening to you wittering and having my shoes dribbled on.'

'We have the calculations,' Commander Grelt announced, ignoring the Doctor. 'We shall calibrate the Eternity Device, and then we will activate it.' He turned to the Doctor at last. 'And you will watch as we bring every fallen Krashok trooper back from the dead. Our army of the undead will be invincible.'

The Doctor returned the Krashok Commander's stare. 'Yawn,' he said.

The Assembly Hall was a vast circular chamber at the centre of the Space Brain. Seats rose up around the edges from a central area where there was a lectern. The back ring of seats had desks in front of them, with computer terminals built into the surface.

Gisella was surprised at how few staff and students there were. They barely filled a quarter of the hall. Most were gathered round the teachers at the back of the hall, examining the screens.

'Cut backs,' Kleb explained. 'We don't get the funding, so there are fewer grants. Parents aren't so keen to give their children the best education when they have to pay a fortune for it.'

Caffey and Kleb introduced Gisella to the teachers, and Mr Gershwinn called them over to look at the screen he was examining.

'Look, the Krashoks are retreating. You can see the life-sign symbols moving back to their ship.'

'Maybe they got what they came for,' Kleb said.

'In which case the Doctor has failed,' Caffey said sadly.

Gisella shook her head. 'The Doctor never fails. He might have had to resort to Plan B, but he hasn't failed.'

'And what is Plan B?' Mr Gershwinn asked.

'It's when he makes it up as he goes along,' Gisella told them. 'Which means he's probably in trouble and needs our help.'

'There's a life sign here that's different to the others,' Miss Renfrew said, leaning over the screen. 'It must be an error. It looks like whoever this is has two hearts.'

'That's the Doctor,' Gisella said. 'And they're taking him to the Krashok ship.' She looked up at the teachers and Kleb and Caffey and the watching children. 'It's time for our own Plan B,' she announced.

'So this would be the way to the Eternity Chamber, would it?' the Doctor asked politely. 'Just down here on the left, I think.'

Commander Grelt glared at him through his cybernetically-enhanced eyes.

'Lucky guess,' the Doctor reassured him. So far his plan, such as it was, was working. He'd managed to distract Grelt enough so that the Doctor hadn't been searched. And he was still alive, which the Doctor had to admit was an unexpected but welcome bonus. Even better, they were actually taking him where he needed to go. Now that the calculations were complete, the Eternity Chamber was the only place the Doctor could stop the Eternity Device from being activated.

There was a downside, of course. Like the fact that he was being held tight by two fierce and deadly Krashoks who would kill him as soon as he tried to escape or to sabotage the Device. But one thing at a time.

Of course, the Doctor had seen the Eternity

Device already with Gisella, so it was easy to pretend he wasn't very impressed. Annoyed, Grelt left him at the back of the chamber with the two guards.

The other Krashoks hurried to control panels and started to shut down the Device so it could be calibrated with the results of the calculations. The Doctor knew he would have just one chance of escape. Just one split-second when he might be able to break free. And then another split-second when he could act.

As the power was disconnected, the Eternity Crystal's glow faded rapidly. The only light in the room came from the monitor screens and the Eternity Device itself. No one had thought to turn on the main lights in the chamber – they simply weren't needed. Not until the Eternity Device powered down.

Then suddenly, apart from the faint glow of the monitor screens at the side of the room, the enormous chamber was plunged into darkness.

Only the Doctor was ready. He felt the grip on his arms slacken slightly as the two Krashok guards realized they couldn't see and needed to switch their visual circuits to infra red. The first split-second.

The Doctor tore himself free, and ran. Not for the exit, but straight for the Eternity Device. If he was right, if he was lucky, he would have another split-second when he could sabotage the device.

The Krashok guards adjusted to the darkness almost at once, and set off after the Doctor. They were closing on him fast as he sprinted across the huge chamber. A clawed hand raked down his coat. Metallic clamps grabbed at his sleeve.

The second split-second – the lights came on.

The Krashoks, operating in the darkness with their night-vision systems were blinded again, this time by the white light flooding into their eyes. In that split-second, the Doctor hurled himself at the Eternity Device, reaching for the Crystal at its heart.

Almost at once, a massive paw slapped him away. A cybernetic hand lifted him down and threw the Doctor to the floor.

Commander Grelt loomed over the Doctor. His tusks glistened as they caught the light. He knew there hadn't been time for the Doctor to tamper with the systems, but he would have them all checked anyway. A full check of the systems before the Eternity Device was powered up.

'You have failed, Doctor,' Grelt rasped. 'Your pathetic plan has come to nothing.' He signalled for the two Krashok guards the Doctor had escaped from to raise their blasters. 'And now you will die.'

Counter-Attack

The Doctor was hauled to his feet. He stared into the barrels of the blasters being levelled at him by the Krashok guards. He closed his eyes. Which was how he missed what happened next.

There was a cry of rage from Commander Grelt. The Doctor opened one eye, and saw that the lights had gone out again. Almost immediately there was a bright flash. Then darkness. Then another bright flash, followed by darkness again.

'Run, Doctor – over here!' a voice called. It was Gisella.

The Krashoks couldn't adjust. If they turned on their infra red vision they were blinded by the frequent flashes of bright light. If they didn't they couldn't see in the dark.

The Doctor couldn't see very well either. But he could hear Gisella calling, and he remembered where the door was. So he ran.

Blaster fire kicked up round his feet. The Krashoks were aiming at the sound of his footsteps as he ran. But their fire was not as accurate as it would be if they could see, and apart from a scalded ankle, the Doctor reached the door unscathed.

'Thanks for that,' he told Gisella.

He beamed at Kleb, Caffey and Mr Gershwinn. And they all ran.

'Magnesium powder,' Kleb explained as they headed back to the Space Brain.

'Liberated from the Chemistry lab, like your smoke bomb solution?'

'That's right,' Kleb said.

'And you ain't seen nothing yet,' Caffey added.

There was a crash from behind them, followed by the sound of heavy blaster fire.

'I think we should hurry,' the Doctor said. 'It sounds like the Krashoks aren't too happy with us. Even though their Eternity Device is ready to go.'

'They're ready to operate it?' Gisella asked, appalled.

'As soon as they've downloaded the calculations.'

'Then I think I know a way we can stop them from the Assembly Hall,' Kleb said.

'We've got to get there first,' the Doctor

pointed out.

'Leave that to us,' Caffey told him.

They reached the main corridor leading to the Assembly Hall. The Krashoks were catching up with them now – angry at the rescue of the Doctor and determined to take revenge.

'They'll catch us before we get there,' the Doctor said. 'I'll give myself up, and buy you time to hack into their systems.'

'No you won't,' Mr Gershwinn said. 'We're ready for them, aren't we?' he said to Gisella, Kleb and Caffey.

'You bet,' Caffey said.

'Sure thing,' Kleb said.

'Leave it to us, Doctor,' Gisella told him.

It was only now that the Doctor noticed the lengths of rope lying across the floor ahead of them. He thought at first they were just discarded – as the Krashoks would believe. But as he got closer, the Doctor saw children drawing back into the shadows of doorways, holding on to the ends of the ropes.

Past the ropes, more children were kneeling down. Some of the floor plates had been removed, and the Doctor could see there was a cavity beneath the floor where cables and pipes ran. He picked his way quickly but carefully across the remaining floor plates, like a hopscotch.

Round the last corner, and there were several more children standing with Professor Apricott, who waved at the Doctor as he raced past. The children were holding buckets, but the Doctor couldn't see what was inside.

There was a long, straight run to the Assembly Hall now. But the Krashoks were gaining fast. The Doctor could guess what would happen when they reached the ropes – any second now.

He heard the shouts and angry cries, and the noise of bodies falling heavily. Then the laughter of children and the sound of running feet. The children had lifted the ropes and held them tight as the Krashoks arrived – tripping the cyborg warriors and sending them flying.

There was a heavy scraping sound now, followed by more running feet. The second lot of children were heaving up the remaining floor plates. Sure enough, moments later there was the sound of battle armour falling heavily on to pipes and cables. The blaster fire intensified – but so too did the sound of laughter.

The Doctor was grinning at his friends as they reached the Assembly Hall. Children were sprinting down the corridor towards them. Some of them held empty buckets and Professor Apricott was looking very pleased with himself.

But they didn't have much of a lead. Already the first Krashoks were rounding the corner – led by a very angry-looking Commander Grelt.

'What was in the buckets?' the Doctor asked as they reached the doors.

Professor Apricott reached them, breathing heavily from running so fast.

'From the kitchens,' he gasped as he struggled to get his breath back.

Over the professor's shoulder, the Doctor saw Commander Grelt raise his blaster. But before he could fire, the Krashok Commander's feet seemed to slide from under him and he crashed into the wall of the corridor. The other Krashoks were also sliding and slipping, going down like pins hit by a bowling ball.

'A mixture of cooking oil and half-set jelly,' Professor Apricott told the Doctor. 'It seems to work very well, don't you think?'

'I do,' the Doctor agreed, standing aside to let the children run past him into the hall. 'It's brilliant. But I think the Krashoks will be more angry than ever now. They won't rest until they kill us all.'

They closed the doors behind them, and the Doctor worked with his sonic screwdriver to seal them shut.

'Won't keep them out for long, I'm afraid,' he said.

Kleb was working urgently at a screen at the back of the hall. The Doctor and the others hurried to join him.

'If I can hack into the Krashok systems in the Physics lab, I can set a computer virus to corrupt their data,' Kleb said. 'They might have finished their calculations, but the answers will be destroyed.'

'Can't they just work it out again?' Gisella asked.

Kleb nodded unhappily. 'But it might buy us some more time to sabotage their equipment.'

There was a hammering from the door, followed by the sound of an explosion from outside. The metal dented and scarred as something heavy hammered into it.

'I'm afraid time is the one thing we don't have,' the Doctor said. 'They'll be through that door any minute!'

Activation!

'The virus is running!' Kleb announced.

At almost the same moment, the door exploded inwards. Metal twisted and buckled, before being blasted across the Assembly Hall. The frame collapsed and the hinges broke away. Through the smoke and flame, a group of Krashoks charged into the Hall.

'We surrender!' the Doctor yelled at once. His voice was full of authority. 'No more killing – we surrender.'

Commander Grelt marched to the central area and stared up at the gathered children and their teachers.

'You are all now prisoners of the Krashoks,' he announced. 'Perhaps we will let you live. Or perhaps not.' His head swung round as he searched for the Doctor and his friends. As soon as he saw them he pointed an armoured hand towards them. 'You, Doctor! You, and your friends will come to our ship for punishment.'

'Ooh,' the Doctor said, 'detention is it? Extra homework? Have to stay late after lessons and go without tea.'

'Silence!' Grelt roared. 'Acting Commander Jorak will deal with you on our ship. Move!'

The Doctor walked calmly down to where Grelt was standing. Gisella, Kleb and Caffey followed.

Gisella signalled for Mr Gershwinn and the other teachers to stay with the children. 'They need you,' she said quietly. 'And the Krashoks don't know you were involved, but they saw Kleb and Caffey.'

In the centre of the Assembly Hall, the Doctor faced Commander Grelt. 'We'll come with you,' he said. 'But you leave these children and their teachers alone. They've given you what you wanted. Now, go and leave them in peace.'

'You think you can give a Krashok Commander *orders*?' Grelt said.

'Oh yes. But if you'd rather see it as a warning, it's all the same to me.'

'You are in no position to give us a warning or issue orders. We will deal with these humans as we see fit.' Grelt turned away.

'Just so we're clear,' the Doctor said, his voice dangerously calm, 'you only get the one warning. No second chance. Leave them alone.'

Grelt turned slowly back. 'You will witness the activation of the Eternity Device. And then you will witness the first act of the great Krashok army that will be reborn – the destruction of this Space Brain and everyone on board. We activate in eight minutes precisely.'

As they were led away, Gisella managed to catch a glimpse of one of the monitor screens on the back row. It showed the progress of the virus as it attacked the Krashok data. She just hoped it would finish its work in time.

Activity

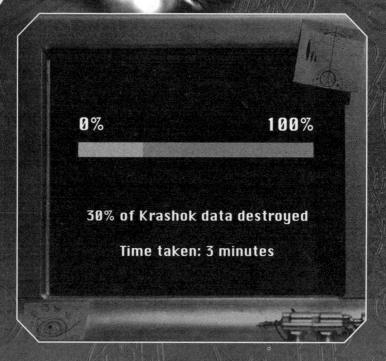

0%   100%

30% of Krashok data destroyed

Time taken: 3 minutes

Will the rest of the Krashok data be destroyed before they activate the Eternity Device in 8 minutes?

Answer _____

Gisella and the Doctor were marched through the Space Brain back to the Krashok ship. Kleb and Caffey were with them.

'I just hope they don't notice what's happening to their data until it's too late to save it,' Kleb whispered.

'I just hope everyone else will be all right,' Caffey whispered back.

'I just hope…' Gisella told them.

She hoped the Doctor had a plan. He was walking along with his head down and his hands in his jacket pockets. If she didn't know better, Gisella might think he was just out for a stroll. But like the rest of them, he was walking to his own execution.

'The virus will work,' Gisella whispered to Kleb when she was sure none of the Krashoks could hear. 'It needed another seven minutes when Commander Grelt said there was eight minutes to activation.'

'There's a lot less than that now,' Kleb pointed out.

They were bundled along the transparent docking tube and back on to the Krashok ship. Then Commander Grelt led the way to the Eternity Chamber.

The Eternity Device was still powered down.

Maybe, Gisella thought, that meant there was a problem.

But Acting Commander Jorak hurried up to Grelt and said: 'All systems have been checked and double-checked. The Eternity Device will be ready for activation as soon as the configuration data is downloaded from the equipment on the Space Brain. The children and staff have done an excellent job. In just a few minutes we will have the data we need.'

The Doctor looked round at the others, and winked. It looked like the virus was working and the Krashoks hadn't even realized.

'Ready to upload the data,' a Krashok announced from one of the control panels. 'Then we can activate the Eternity Device and focus the energy of the Eternity Crystal to bring back our warriors from the dead.'

'Excellent!' Commander Grelt said.

'But…' the Krashok technician went on, 'there is a problem.'

Commander Grelt froze like a statue. Then very slowly he turned to look at the Doctor, Gisella, Caffey and Kleb. 'What problem?'

'A computer software virus has been introduced

into the Space Brain networks. It was programmed to hunt down and destroy our data.'

Grelt was shaking with anger. His tusks quivered. 'Did it find the data?'

'It did.'

There was silence. The Doctor grinned. Gisella felt suddenly light-headed and full of hope. Caffey and Kleb both laughed.

Then the Krashok technician said: 'But I anticipated such an action. The data the virus found and destroyed was a copy. The real data has been quarantined in a safe partition on our own computers.' The technician raised a hand that was encased in a clawed, metal gauntlet. 'The data is now complete. The Eternity Device can be activated at once.'

'We failed,' Kleb said.

Caffey put her arm round his shoulders. 'You did your best.'

The Doctor pulled himself up to his full height. 'You had your last warning, Commander Grelt,' he said. 'But I'm telling you one more time – don't activate the Eternity Device.'

Comander Grelt ignored him. 'Are all the check sequences and preliminary stages complete?' he asked.

Acting Commader Jorak nodded. 'They are. All checks confirm the Device is one hundred per cent ready.'

Grelt turned to look at the Doctor as he spoke his next words. His mouth curled into a smile of satisfaction and victory. 'Then activate the Eternity Device.'

The room was suddenly humming with power. The Eternity Device began to glow with energy. The Crystal at its heart was burning bright.

Gisella watched in both awe and fear. After all she and the Doctor and their many friends had been through to prevent this moment ever arriving, the Krashoks had won.

The End of Eternity

Commander Grelt gave a roar of laughter. Beside him, Acting Commander Jorak was staring transfixed at the Eternity Device.

'I'm sorry,' the Doctor said as the Eternity Crystal blazed with blue light. 'I am so sorry.' He shook his head sadly and looked at the floor as if ashamed, his hands thrust deep in his pockets.

'Don't worry,' Gisella said.

'It's not your fault,' Caffey told him.

'We did our best,' Kleb agreed.

The Doctor looked up. 'I wasn't talking to you,' he said. 'I was talking to the Krashoks.' He turned to Grelt, who had stopped laughing. 'I'm so very sorry,' the Doctor said again. 'Why didn't you listen?'

Grelt's expression changed from triumph to confusion as the Doctor took his hand from his pocket. He was holding a large Crystal, about the size of an egg.

'I swapped the real Eternity Crystal for the fake again, when you thought I was trying to sabotage the Device. You really should have dismantled it and run a full test.'

'The readings are not what we predicted,' the Krashok technician shouted across the Eternity Chamber. 'The power is building too fast. We won't get the steady stream of energy we need, we'll get a sudden blast.'

Grelt was shaking with fury. 'Then everyone will die. Even you, Doctor and your friends.'

The Doctor shook his head. 'I'm afraid not. Well, actually, I'm not afraid at all. You see, you configured the Eternity Device to work only on Krashoks. Otherwise you'd be bringing back everyone and everything from the dead, remember? Only now, without the real Crystal to focus the energy that blast will affect only the life form you configured the Device for.'

'It will destroy the Krashoks,' Gisella realized.

'You have to stop it!' Acting Commander Jorak yelled.

The technicians were already working frantically at the controls. The chief technician looked up.

He shook his armour-plated head.

'Help us!' Jorak roared at the Doctor.

'I tried,' he said quietly. 'I offered Grelt a chance. And he refused it. Maybe you should talk to him about that.'

Jorak turned abruptly to Grelt. But the Commander was holding his head in his hands. A tear dripped off the end of one of his tusks.

The Doctor sighed. He tossed the Eternity Crystal from one hand to the other, then flung it into the heart of the glowing Device. 'The one thing that can destroy it,' he told Gisella. 'Your father Varlos knew that all along, of course.'

'So what do we do now?' Caffey asked.

'Gisella knows,' the Doctor said.

'Gisella?' Kleb prompted.

Gisella smiled. 'Run!'

The Krashoks didn't try to stop them. They were now all clutching at their heads, like Commander Grelt, as the power from the Eternity Device flooded into their brains. Service robots stood silent and still, waiting for orders that would never come.

As soon as they were back through the docking tube, the Doctor closed and locked the airlock door.

'They can just open it again from the other side,'

Kleb pointed out.

'It isn't to keep the Krashoks out,' the Doctor said. 'It's to keep the air in, when their ship explodes.'

'It'll explode?' Caffey said, looking out of the big window behind the Principal's desk.

'What about the Krashoks in the Assembly Hall?' Gisella wondered.

'What indeed,' the Doctor replied. 'Let's go and find out.'

'You have condemned us all!' Acting Commander Jorak shouted above the noise of the Eternity Device as the power continued to build. 'You are no longer fit to command the Krashoks. You will die disgraced and demoted. A mere trooper. This I – Commander Jorak, of the great Krashok Empire – decree.'

He stepped away from Grelt and gave a battle salute. Then he turned away, not wanting to see his former Commander as they both died.

The energy ripped out from the Eternity Device. It burned into the Krashoks, disintegrating their flesh and bone and reducing them to dust.

Only things that were not organic Krashok survived. Empty space armour fell to the floor.

Trophies and medals and insignia clattered beside the armour. Dull grey dust fell like snow across the Krashok ship.

It was the same in the Assembly Hall. The Doctor and his friends arrived in time to see a suit of armour topple forward. A cloud of dust fell from the empty helmet. A cybernetic eye-piece smashed on the ground.

All around, the Krashoks left to guard the children and staff disintegrated. Dust hung in the air like smoke.

Then the whole Space Brain shook violently as the Eternity Device exploded – taking the entire Krashok ship with it.

'Play your cards right,' the Doctor said to Caffey and Kleb in the silence that followed, 'and you might get an extra long lunch break while this gets tidied up.'

All too soon, it was time for goodbyes. Caffey, Kleb and Mr Gershwinn walked with the Doctor and Gisella back to the TARDIS.

'Where will you go?' Kleb wondered. 'What will you do?'

The Doctor shrugged. 'Here and there. This and that. One thing and another. Well,' he decided, 'another thing then one more, likely. What do you think, Gisella?'

'I think,' she said slowly, 'that I'll stay here, actually.'

'What?' the Doctor said. 'What?' He took a step backwards. 'What?!'

Gisella laughed. 'Is it such a surprise? There is so much to learn, and this is the absolute best place to do it. My father is dead, and his work is ended. Our adventure is over, Doctor.'

'Oh, but there are so many more adventures just waiting to happen.'

'Come back and tell me about them,' Gisella said. 'One day, when you have a minute or two to spare – if that ever happens – come back and tell me of your adventures. And maybe, by then, I'll be ready for another one. If you'll let me.'

The Doctor smiled. 'Oh Gisella, you know you'll always be welcome. We had such fun, didn't we? We were so great. So fantastic.'

'We'll look after her, Doctor,' Mr Gershwinn said. 'She can stay here as long as she wants. Maybe even become a teacher when she grows up.

We'll look after her.'

The Doctor and Gisella both laughed.

'What's so funny?' Caffey asked.

'Gisella's older than she looks,' the Doctor said. 'Older than any of you – and that includes you, Mr Gershwinn. She'll look after you, not the other way round.'

'Even so,' Gisella said, 'I'll be the best student ever.' She glanced at Caffey and Kleb. 'Well, maybe with a couple of exceptions. But I'll do my best.'

'Course you will,' the Doctor said. 'You'll be brilliant!'

Then, quickly, before he showed them just how sad he was, the Doctor opened the TARDIS doors and stepped inside.

'Absolutely brilliant!' his muffled voice said from inside the TARDIS.

Then with a grating, rasping sound, the TARDIS faded away.

'Oh, you are kidding,' Kleb said.

'No,' Gisella told him. 'That's just the Doctor, off to another adventure.'

'Cool!' Caffey said.

TARDIS
Data Bank
The Krashoks

The Krashok are a race dedicated to developing weapons which they then sell on. It is in their interest to keep wars going — or even start them — so they can sell arms to both sides. They remain strictly neutral unless forced into action. But of course the Krashok have access to all the most terrible weapons.

Their ambition was always to build their own empire, and to do this they contracted the fabled Darksmith Collective to build the so-called Eternity Device. This would revitalize injured Krashok troops, and even bring back their dead warriors, restored to life and ready to fight again.

The Krashoks are themselves cyborgs — humanoid, but 'enhanced' to be the ultimate soldiers. They travel the universe, searching for the most ferocious predators, the most successful fighters, taking the best bits from what they found and adding it to their own armoury.